Grandma's Purple Flowers

ADJOA J. BURROWES

LEE & LOW BOOKS Inc.
New York

LEE & LOW BOOKS Inc., 95 Madison Avenue, New York, NY 10016 leeandlow.com
Manufactured in China by South China Printing Co. Book design by Christy Hale Book production by The Kids at Our House
The text is set in Barmeno. The illustrations are rendered using a cut-paper collage technique that incorporates watercolors and acrylics.
First Edition Library of Congress Cataloging-in-Publication Data Burrowes, Adjoa J. Grandma's purple flowers / Adjoa J. Burrowes.– 1st ed.
p. cm. ISBN 978-1-880000-73-1 (hardcover) ISBN 978-1-60060-343-3 (paperback) I. Title. PZ7.B94534 Gr 2000 00-035414
(HC) 10 9 8 7 6 5 4 3 2
(PB) 10 9 8 7 6 5 4 3 2 1

To my children—Kassahun, Hyacinth and Hilary—A.J.B.

My favorite Grandma
lives through the park
and down the hill.
Momma lets me go visit her
all the time.

A big hug and a smile
are always waiting
at Grandma's house.

Skipping through the park in summer,
the sun winks at me.

I spin round and round,
throwing kisses to the sun.

I stop and pick purple flowers,
all kinds of purple flowers—
Grandma's favorites.

I pluck some daisies, too,
and make a crown for my head.
I pretend I'm a flower princess.
Hyacinth is my name.

Grandma opens the squeaky door.
“Hi, Sweetie Pie,” she says, smiling.

When Grandma sees the purple flowers,
her smile grows wide,
like the Mississippi River
where Grandma and I sometimes sit.

There are two gold teeth
in Grandma's mouth.
One has the shape
of the moon in it,
the other, a star.

Grandma says that down south
where she grew up,
those were for good luck.

Grandma puts the flowers
in a vase by the window,
next to a picture of me
when I was little.

Later we eat soft corn muffins,
so sweet and yummy.

Walking through the park in fall,
the leaves show off
their carnival colors.
The bright oranges and reds
perform over my head.

After the show,
the leaves spin to the ground,
twirling this way and that.
“Hurray! Hurray!” I shout,
crunching the leaves under my feet,
on my way to Grandma’s.

Grandma lets me rake the leaves
in the backyard garden
we planted together.
"Why do leaves have to fall and die?" I ask.
"Everything has its time," Grandma tells me.

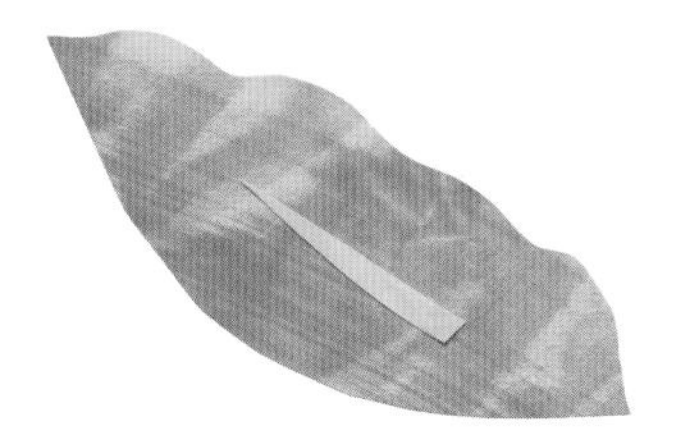

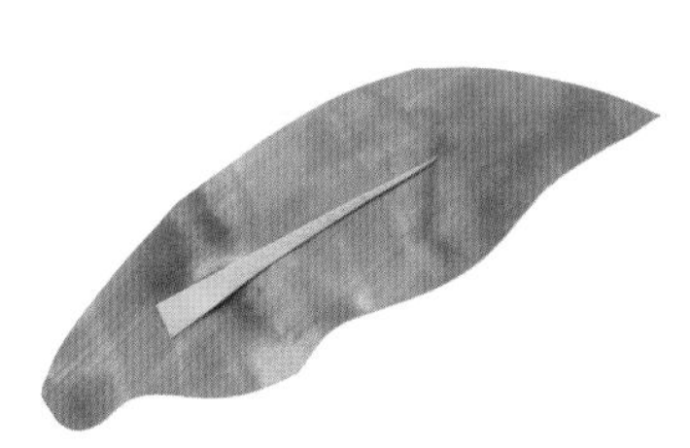

We go inside for a slice of pecan pie.
Afterwards, Grandma lets me
comb her hair.
Before long, she dozes off
and I twist her hair
into a ball of silver.

When winter comes,
cottony snowflakes
dance around me
as I walk through the park
and down the hill
to Grandma's house.

I plod through the snow
bundled in my snowsuit
and the scarf that Grandma made.
The bare branches above
stretch out like long fingers
reaching for the sun.

With almost-frozen fingers
I knock on Grandma's door.
"Please open up!" I shout,
shivering.
But she doesn't answer.

I knock again, louder,
and peek through the window.

Grandma slowly comes to the door,
sipping sassafras tea.
“That smells funny, Grandma,” I say,
“like root beer.”
Grandma is silent.
Her slippered feet shuffle across the floor
real slow.

“Grandma, can we bake
corn muffins?” I ask.
“No, Baby,” she says softly.
“I’m feeling too tired today.”
Her quiet eyes stare straight at mine.

I put my arms around her
and give her a great big hug.

Grandma rubs my back gently
and braids my hair
that has come undone.
“Baby, you’re gettin’ so grown up,”
she says.

Grandma passed away that night.
When Momma tells me
the next morning, I cry and cry.
I want to stay in my room
for the rest of the winter,
but Momma won't let me.

Oh, how I miss Grandma!

Walking through the park
makes me sad.
The once-bright snow is now
dirty and gray.

Skinny branches make
spooky shadows on the ground.
The icy wind whips past me.
I can't wait for spring.

One day I wake up
to a branch tapping
on my window.

Outside all the branches
sway in the breeze,
dotted with baby buds.

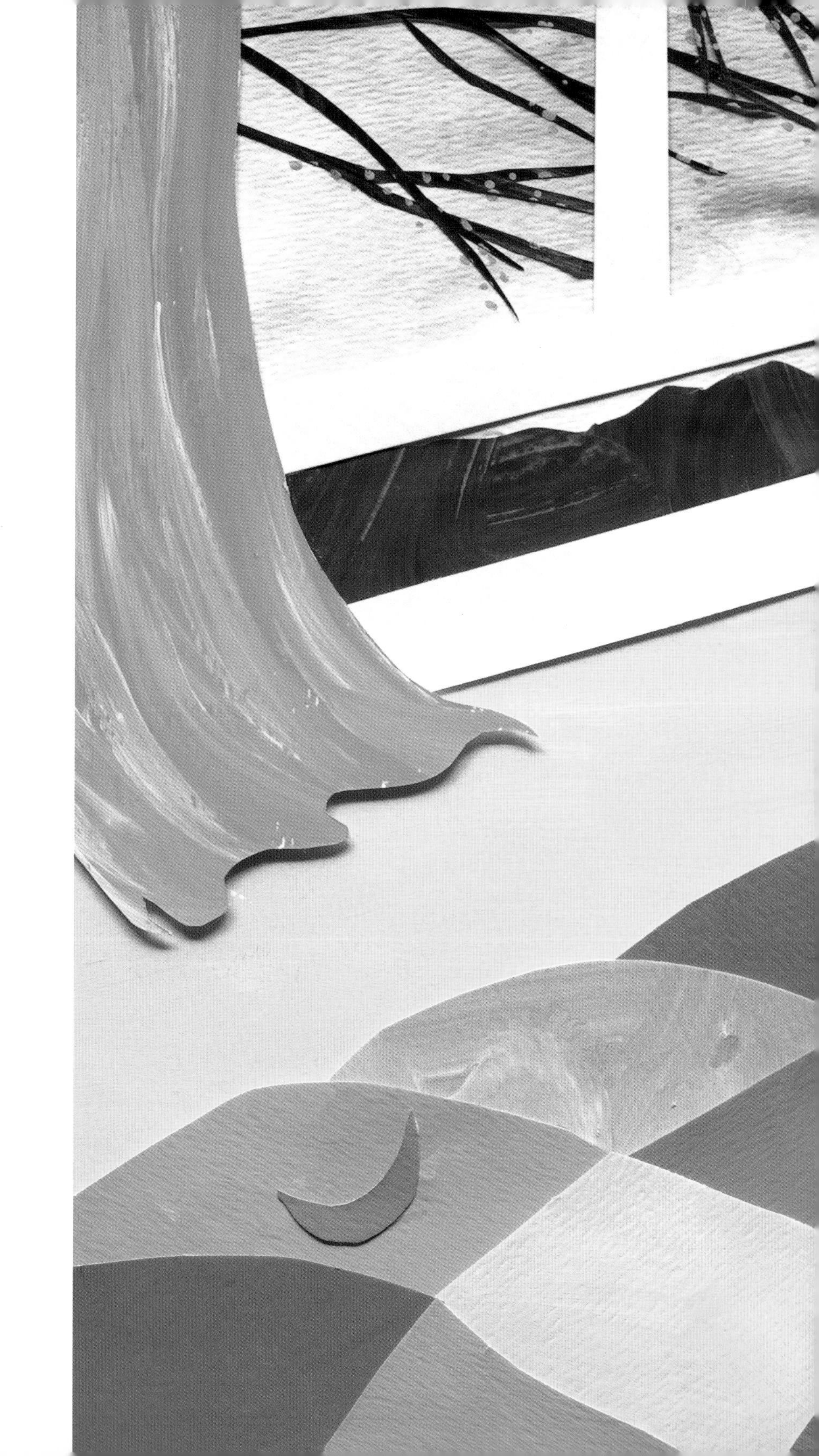

“Spring has finally come!” I shout.

I dash outside
and run as fast as I can
through the park
and down the hill.

A leaf circles to the ground
in back of Grandma's house
where we used to plant
collard greens and okra.

When I look closely
I see tiny purple flowers
shooting up from the ground,
stretching to the sky.

My heart feels happy,
but part of me still wants to cry.
I hug my shoulders like
Grandma would,
and feel a little better.

Whenever I see purple flowers now
I think of Grandma.
I feel her big hug,
and I smile wide—
like the Mississippi River.